THREE CLASSIC ADVENTURES OF
SUPERTATO

by Sue Hendra and Paul Linnet

SIMON & SCHUSTER

London New York Sydney Toronto New Delhi

Brilliant librarians and fabulous teachers

TO THE RESCUE!

SIMON & SCHUSTER
First published in Great Britain in 2020
by Simon & Schuster UK Ltd
First Floor, 222 Gray's Inn Road, London, WC1X 8HB
A CBS Company

Supertato: **Veggies Assemble** first published in 2016
Supertato: **Run, Veggies, Run!** first published in 2017
Supertato: **Evil Pea Rules** first published in 2017

A CIP catalogue record for this book is available from the British Library

978-1-4711-9183-1 (PB)
978-1-4711-9184-8 (eBook)

Printed in China

1 3 5 7 9 10 8 6 4 2

SUPERTATO

VEGGIES ASSEMBLE

It was night-time in the supermarket and everyone was sleeping peacefully ... or were they?

Someone was looking for trouble.
"**Mwah ha ha ha ha**, soon this supermarket will be mine, **ALL** mine!"

And with one **click**,
ALL the freezers were switched off.

GASP!

FREEZERS

ON

OFF

You may already know this, but some vegetables are frozen for a very good reason. If they defrost they turn bad – really bad.

And baddest of them all is The Evil Pea!

"Wakey wakey!" he called.

One evil pea is bad enough.

But now there were BAGS of them!

The supermarket was in meltdown.
"Run for it!" panicked Pepper.

"S...S...SAVE ME!"
stuttered Pear.

"SAVE ME!"
begged Melon.

"SAVE ME!"
cried Carrot.

"I'M MELTING!"
pleaded Lolly.
"And time's running out!"

Was there anyone
who could save them?

But, before Supertato could save anyone,
he was attacked by a swarm of peas!

"What's going on?" asked Aubergine.
"We're DOOMED, that's what!" cried Cucumber.

Things were going from bad to worse.

"I'm going . . .
to need . . .
some . . .
backup.
If I can just . . .
call the . . ."

CLICK!

They used ninja know-how!

HI-YA!

HONEY

They used MASSIVE muscles!

Hrrr!

They used
fancy footwork.

And they used a box
with a door cut in it.

PEA PARTY

But what about the lollies? And where was Supertato?

"Sorry I'm late, I just needed to pick up some dessert!"

... Hmmmmmmmmppfff!"

"You're going to do what?" asked Supertato.

"Three cheers for Supertato!" shouted Broccoli. Supertato blushed. "I couldn't have done it without the Superveggies."

"Actually, I'm not a vegetable, I'm a fruit," said Tomato. And everybody laughed and cheered.

So, with the peas back in their bags
and the freezers locked . . .

... the supermarket was once again a safe place to be.

"Isn't it wonderful," said one lolly to the other. "We're all back to normal again!"

SUPERTATO

RUN, VEGGIES, RUN!

It was night-time in the supermarket but Supertato and the veggies were going for the burn.

"Come on, veggies, you can do it!"

"To keep fit of course! Whoever heard of an unhealthy vegetable?" Supertato grinned.

"Just look at yourselves!
It's time we got you fruit and veggies into shape."

Supertato thought for a minute. "I know – let's have a sports day!" he said.

Everyone groaned.

"There'll be prizes . . ."

Everyone cheered!

"ATTENTION!" shouted Supertato as they all limbered up. "It's time for the first events. Running and jumping and spinning.

Asparagus, you can be the starter."

GO PEPPER!

Then suddenly the ground shook.

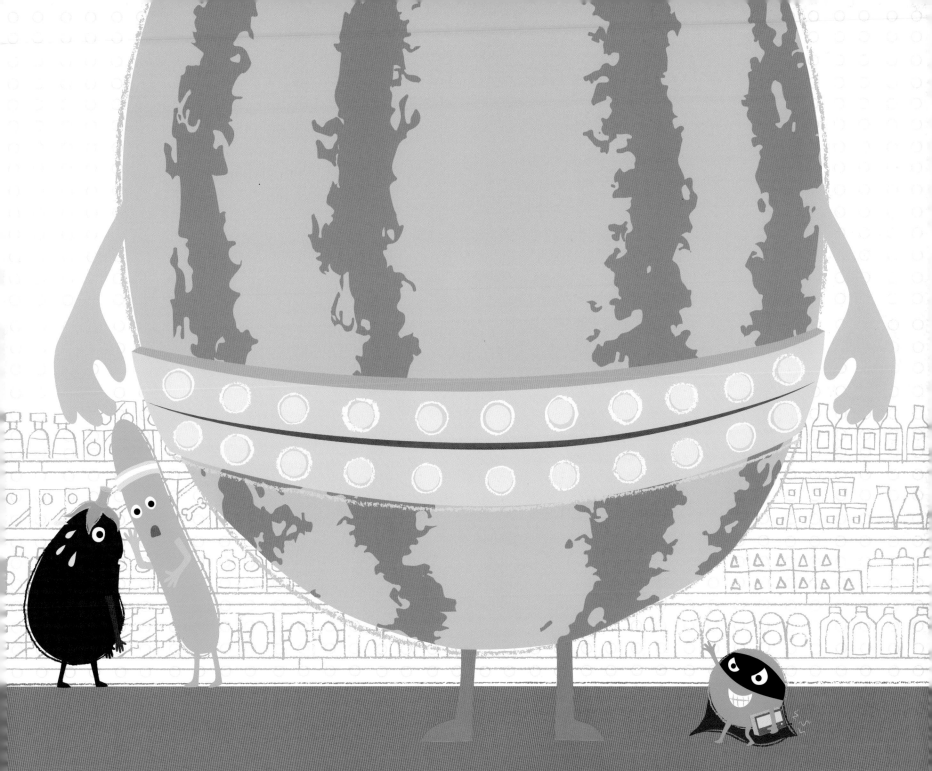

"Oh no," said Cucumber. "It's **The Evil Pea!**"

Everyone gasped. The Evil Pea was grinning.
"Gloria here wishes to enter your competition," he said.

"A pleasure to meet you, Gloria," said Supertato.

CRUSH OPPONENTS
WIN PRIZES WIN PRIZES
PRIZES PRIZES

"Hmmm,"
thought Supertato.

"Ok, let's start the race.

Carrot, you're in lane one,
Broccoli lane two,
Cucumber lane three,
Gloria . . . you can take four, five and six.

Over to you, Asparagus."

"They will never defeat my robot," sniggered The Evil Pea. "Those prizes are as good as mine!

Mwah ha ha ha ha!"

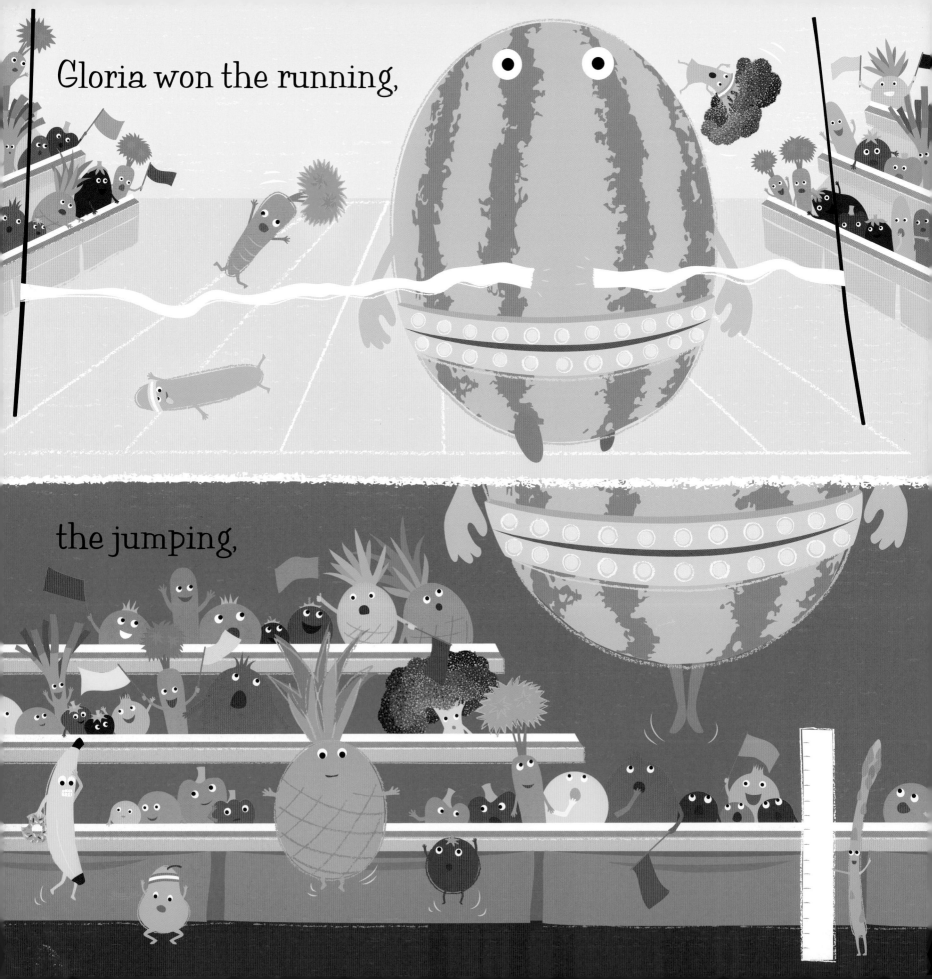

Gloria won the running,

the jumping,

the spinning,

and the lifting of heavy things.

In fact, she won
everything!

"Time to be off, Gloria," said The Evil Pea. "We have all the prizes, our work here is done!"

"Well, actually," said Supertato, "there's one more event to go . . .

"STOP!" shrieked The Evil Pea. "I don't think you should be doing any swimming, Gloria.

You're not really a **water** melon!"

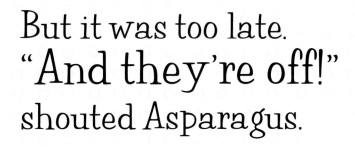

But it was too late. "And they're off!" shouted Asparagus.

Gloria was well in the lead . . .

...but then she started crackling and sparking...

... and juggling!

He scooped up the swimmers and took them to safety.

"Hurray for Supertato!"

But just as Supertato
flew back in to deal with
the melonbot . . .

. . . IT EXPLODED!

"Is this the end for Supertato?"
panicked the pineapples.

"Oooh," said The Evil Pea, "time for a 100-metre dash."

"Not so fast, Pea. There are no prizes for cheating.

It's back to the freezer for you!"

"It's a good thing we've seen the last of that naughty melonbot ..." said one fish finger to another.

WIN PRIZES
ZZZZZ I'LL BE BACK ....

SUPERTATO

EVIL PEA RULES

The Evil Pea sat upon his icy throne.
He was king of everything that he could see.

Unfortunately . . .

... all he could see was the inside of a boring old freezer! And he'd had enough of it.

It was night-time in the supermarket and all the good little veggies were settling down to sleep.

But this little veggie wasn't sleepy at all.

"*Hmmmmpfff!*" cried the cucumbers.

"Oh NO!" mouthed the melons. "He's escaped! The Evil Pea is back!"

"**Of course I'm back!**" shrieked the pea.
"Now how about a lovely haircut?"

Who could save these
poor pineapples in peril?
Supertato, that's who!

"FREEZE!" he shouted.
"You're coming with me!"

And before the Evil Pea
could get snippy . . .

… he was popped back into the freezer where he belonged.

The pea was furious.

"FREEZE, EH?
I'll give him FREEZE!

I'll give them ALL FREEZE!"

DANGER

And within seconds he was out of the freezer and up to no good.

Hrrrrrrr

The Evil Pea had a plan. It was his **craftiest** one yet.

With his pretend veggies in one hand and a freezy jet at the ready, he shouted in his best veggie voice . . .

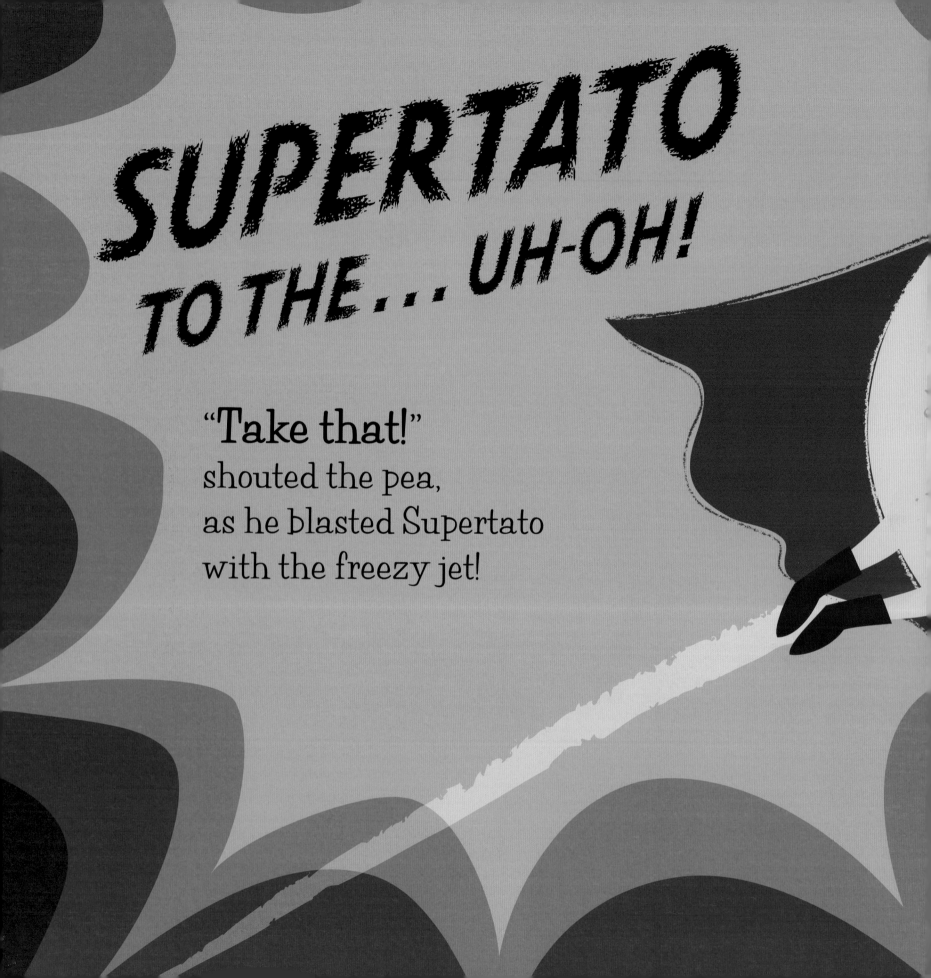

SUPERTATO
TO THE ... UH-OH!

"Take that!"
shouted the pea,
as he blasted Supertato
with the freezy jet!

"Time to chill out, Super**lolly**," cackled the Evil Pea. "What is it you always say? Some vegetables are frozen for a very good reason!

Mwah ha ha ha ha!"

And with that he zoomed off over aisles of sleeping veggies . . .

. . . to get ready for part two of his evil plan.

Operation Freezification.

He ripped all the pipes from
the freezers and

WHOOSH!

An icy blast filled the supermarket.
"By morning this supermarket will be

mine all mine!"

When the veggies woke up,
they couldn't believe their eyes.

Everywhere they looked, there was ice and snow.

"*Mwah ha ha ha ha!*" squealed the Evil Pea.

"How do you like the supermarket now, you nitwits?"

"WE LOVE IT!" cheered the veggies.

"NO! ... NO! ... NO!

It's not supposed to be FUN!"

Meanwhile our hero was still in a fix.
Luckily, the hot chillies had a plan.

"Quick everyone,
GROUP HUG!"

"Oooh, that should break the ice!"
said one pineapple to another.

And they were right!
Soon our hero was free . . .

And going on a – shopping spree?

"I'll be needing one of these ...

one of these ...

... and definitely one of these."

"Ho-ho-hold it right there, Pea!" called Supertato.

"No sloping off for you.
We need to find out who's been
nice and who's been naughty . . .

. . . as if I didn't know."

Everyone snuggled up on the sleigh.
"What a lovely tree," said Supertato.
"There's just one thing missing . . ."

"Merry Christmas, Pea," said Supertato.

"I know you're no angel.
But everyone's got to
start somewhere!"

SUPERTATO
Sue Hendra & Paul Linnet

SUPERTATO
VEGGIES ASSEMBLE

SUPERTATO
RUN, VEGGIES, RUN!

SUPERTATO
EVIL PEA RULES!

SUPERTATO
VEGGIES IN THE VALLEY OF DOOM
Sue Hendra & Paul Linnet

SUPERTATO
CARNIVAL

If you like

SUPERTATO

you'll love these other

adventures from

Sue Hendra & Paul Linnet

BARRY
THE FISH WITH FINGERS
Sue Hendra & Paul Linnet

BARRY
THE FISH WITH FINGERS
AND THE HAIRY SCARY MONSTER
Sue Hendra & Paul Linnet

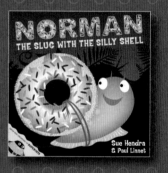

NORMAN
THE SLUG WITH THE SILLY SHELL
Sue Hendra & Paul Linnet

THE SLUG WHO SAVED CHRISTMAS
Sue Hendra & Paul Linnet

NO-BOT
THE ROBOT WITH NO BOTTOM!
SUE HENDRA & PAUL LINNET

GORDON'S GREAT ESCAPE
Sue Hendra & Paul Linnet

KEITH
THE CAT WITH THE MAGIC HAT
Sue Hendra & Paul Linnet

Sue Hendra & Paul Linnet

I NEED A WEE!